The Odyssey

Retold from Homer original
by Tania Zamorsky

Illustrated by Eric Freeberg

STERLING CHILDREN'S BOOKS
New York

STERLING CHILDREN'S BOOKS
New York

An Imprint of Sterling Publishing
387 Park Avenue South
New York, NY 10016

STERLING CHILDREN'S BOOKS and the distinctive Sterling Children's Books logo are
trademarks of Sterling Publishing Co., Inc.

Text © 2011 by Tania Zamorsky
Illustrations © 2011 by Eric Freeberg

Classic Starts is a trademark of Sterling Publishing Co., Inc.

ISBN 978-1-4027-7334-1

Library of Congress Cataloging-in-Publication Data

Zamorsky, Tania.
   The odyssey / retold from Homer original by Tania Zamorsky ; illustrated by Eric
Freeberg.
      p. cm. — (Classic starts)
   ISBN 978-1-4027-7334-1
   1. Odysseus (Greek mythology)—Juvenile literature. I. Freeberg, Eric.
II. Homer. Odyssey. III. Title.
   BL820.O3Z36 2011
   398.20938'02—dc22

                                                                        2010039927

Distributed in Canada by Sterling Publishing
$^c/o$ Canadian Manda Group, 165 Dufferin Street
Toronto, Ontario, Canada M6K 3H6
Distributed in the United Kingdom by GMC Distribution Services
Castle Place, 166 High Street, Lewes, East Sussex, England BN7 1XU
Distributed in Australia by Capricorn Link (Australia) Pty. Ltd.
P.O. Box 704, Windsor, NSW 2756, Australia

For information about custom editions, special sales, and premium and
corporate purchases, please contact Sterling Special Sales at 800-805-5489
or specialsales@sterlingpublishing.com.

Manufactured in China
Lot#:
8 10 9 7
03/14

www.sterlingpublishing.com/kids.

CONTENTS

✂

Prologue

This is the story of a great hero named Odysseus, king of Ithaca, who won victory in the famous Trojan War. He was the leader of a great many men. His soldiers fought beside him and were very loyal to him.

This was a time when gods and goddesses roamed and ruled the earth. The home of the gods was Mount Olympus. From up there, the gods watched humans struggle down on earth. Among them was Zeus, king of the gods, with his children Athena and Hermes. Athena was the goddess of wisdom, strength, and war. Hermes was the messenger of the gods. There was also Aphrodite, the goddess of love, and Hera, the goddess of women and marriage. Poseidon was god of the sea. Sometimes the gods got involved in human lives.

Odysseus and his soldiers angered some of the gods during the Trojan War. Because of this, the gods decided to make Odysseus's voyage home very long and rough. It became a winding journey—an odyssey—that took Odysseus ten years. Along the way, he and his men passed many islands and met many creatures. Some of the creatures were good and some were bad. Some of them were helpful and some of them meant to harm Odysseus and his men. But Odysseus was lucky. He was helped by the goddess Athena. She took pity on him.

But the best stories start at the beginning. So, then, shall ours.

⌒

The Trojan War began because of love, jealousy, and betrayal. One day Zeus was hosting a wedding banquet on Mount Olympus. All the gods, half gods, and royal people were invited, except for Eris, the goddess of trouble. As revenge for this, Eris came in disguise and threw an apple down onto the banquet table. It was a gift, she claimed, for the fairest goddess in the room.

Athena, Hera, and Aphrodite began to fight over the apple. They asked Zeus to decide who was to get the fruit. Zeus was smarter than that, and refused. Instead, he named a young mortal man to be the judge. His name was Paris, and he was from the city of Troy.

The three goddesses began to bargain with the young man. Hera offered Paris power over lands far and wide. Athena promised him wisdom, strength, and courage. But Aphrodite offered the young man the best prize of all. She promised the love of the most beautiful mortal woman in the world. The young man chose Aphrodite as the fairest goddess of the three. Aphrodite enjoyed her apple.

The most beautiful woman in the world was Helen. She was already married to King Menelaus of Sparta. But Paris didn't care. He went to Menelaus's castle and took Helen back to his home in Troy.

Menelaus was furious. So was King Agamemnon, his brother. They set out to take back Helen. Menelaus and Agamemnon took many other men with them, including Odysseus. This group of mighty kings and their soldiers was called the Acheans. They sailed their great ships to the coast of Troy. This is how the Trojan War began. It lasted ten years.

After years of struggle, the Acheans were finally victorious over the Trojans! Helen was reunited with her true husband, Menelaus. In this final year of the war, Odysseus came up with a plan to destroy the city of Troy and end the war completely. He directed his men to build a giant, hollow wooden horse and told them to climb inside. Odysseus joined them in hiding. The horse was pulled to Troy's city gates and left just outside.

There was a note around the horse's neck. It said that the creature was an offering from Odysseus to the goddess Athena. It also said that his army had left Troy. The Trojans were thrilled to find the horse at their gates. To them, it meant the Achean army had given up. The

Trojans dragged the beautiful carved creature into the center of their city. They threw a big party to celebrate winning the war.

Odysseus and his men waited until night arrived and the moon was full. Then they crept out of the giant horse and attacked the celebrating Trojans. The Trojans, who were surprised by the attack, had no chance. Odysseus and his men won the battle and destroyed the city of Troy.

With the war finally over, Agamemnon, Menelaus, and Helen set sail for Sparta. The other Achean kings and soldiers also left to journey home. It had been a long and awful war, and they were ready for peace again.

But the Acheans had angered some of the gods during the Trojan War. The soldiers' greed and violence enraged them. The soldiers had destroyed many temples to the gods in the city of Troy. This was not allowed. Because of this, the gods decided that the men would have difficult journeys after the war. The travelers faced severe storms and many shipwrecks. Many of them died trying to get home.

Odysseus desperately wanted to go home, too. After all, he and his soldiers had enjoyed a great victory. He wanted to celebrate with his friends and family. He could not wait another hour to see his wife, Penelope, and his son, Telemachus. But he, too, had a very long and difficult journey ahead of him.

And we shall join him.

CHAPTER 1

Odysseus and Penelope

⌒

Picture a man sitting on the shore of a beautiful island. The sand is white. The water and endless sky are a brilliant blue. At his side is a beautiful goddess, named Calypso. She loves him and wants him to stay with her forever on this island. Some men would be happy with this, but not this one. This man stares out onto the water. His heart is troubled, and his mind is very far away.

This man is Odysseus. He is dreaming of a land very far away: Ithaca. It is his home, where his wife, Penelope, and his son, Telemachus, still

live. He needs to find his way back to that place. He would do anything to be there again.

～⌒ᴼ

Penelope sat on her balcony at her beautiful home back in Ithaca. She stared out into the distance. It was a dark night. A vast ocean separated her from her husband, Odysseus. He had been gone for many years, fighting in the Trojan War. Even though the war had been over for ten years already, Odysseus still had not come home. Yet Penelope had hope that he was alive. She knew her husband was a great, strong man. He would return one day. He simply had to.

In the meantime, Penelope had troubles of her own. It was true—Odysseus had been gone for a very long time. Many people in Ithaca thought he might be dead and that Penelope should find a new husband.

Her trouble started slowly—at first just a couple of suitors arrived. Soon, though, her husband's house was full of suitors. Each man wanted Penelope to become his wife. These suitors were the sons of Ithaca's finest men. They were educated, athletic, and clever. Each of them hoped that Penelope would choose him as her husband.

But Penelope decided she could not yet move on. She would not choose another husband. Penelope loved Odysseus too much. And anyway, she had a feeling her husband was still alive. The suitors quickly grew impatient and nasty.

While Penelope stayed in her rooms upstairs, the suitors lounged around all day throughout Odysseus's enormous house. They only went home late at night and returned early every morning. The men made themselves quite at home. They relaxed on fine couches and ordered the servants to bring them food and drink.

But Penelope was clever, too. She began to work on a big needlework project. She was making a great tapestry to hang on her wall, in honor of her husband. It contained threads of fancy gold and silver, deep blue and fiery red. Penelope sent word to the suitors. She *would* choose one of them to marry, she told them— as soon as she had sewn her last stitch.

All day she sewed. This pleased the suitors and bought her more time. But at night she would sit by candlelight and secretly undo her stitches.

On this night, Penelope sat on the balcony, taking out the stitches she had made that day. The winds that came off the ocean created a sad melody. She wept for Odysseus. She let her mind imagine what kind of beautiful tapestry she could make one day, and not have to undo, to honor her husband.

CHAPTER 2

Athena Helps Odysseus

The gods had started to feel sorry for Odysseus. They sat high up on Mount Olympus discussing him. Some of them took pity on him, especially the goddess Athena. She had always been fond of Odysseus. Athena hated watching him struggle to make his way home for ten years.

"Just imagine how lonely he must be, stuck on that island so far away from home," said Athena. "I know Odysseus has made mistakes. He has angered us at times, but I think he has suffered long enough. We should help him to get home."

"He *has* been very generous to us in the past," agreed Zeus. He reminded the gods of Odysseus's many sacrifices to them.

Poseidon disagreed. "He blinded my son, the king of the Cyclopes! He does not deserve to return home," he growled.

But Zeus was king of the gods, and his choice ruled over all. He decided to send Athena to Ithaca, disguised as a human. She would speak with Odysseus's son, Telemachus. To help bring Odysseus home sooner, she would make Telemachus feel brave and instruct the boy to search for his father.

Athena leaped up and put on her golden sandals. She flew down from the top of Mount Olympus. When she arrived at Odysseus's house, she saw Penelope's suitors lying about. They ate and drank until their stomachs were stuffed.

The men littered the floors of Odysseus's home with scraps of food. They spilled their drinks all over the beautiful carpets and chairs. They gave orders to the servants, who ran around fulfilling their wishes. Athena was shocked.

The goddess, disguised as an older man, saw Telemachus standing in the corner, looking miserable.

"Do you recognize me, Telemachus?" she asked. "I am an old friend of your father's."

Telemachus forced a smile. "My father's friends are always welcome here," he said. "But not these men!" Telemachus shouted to the crowd of suitors. Not one paid attention to him.

He turned to Athena. "I apologize for my outburst, sir. But I am very upset. These suitors will not leave, and I cannot make them. They sit here all day, eating our food and disrespecting my father's house. I am at my wit's end! If only my father were to come back. Then these evil men would go away. But I've given up hope that I will ever see my father again."

"Dear Telemachus," Athena said gently. "You are a smart, strong young man. It is time to show Ithaca what you are made of."

"But how?" Telemachus asked.

"Go to the town hall and call a meeting of the assembly," Athena said. "You must ask the town's leadership for help. Invite the suitors. At the end of the meeting, order them to leave your home."

The next day, Telemachus went to the town hall where Ithaca's leaders sat. When he arrived, he requested a meeting. The suitors were called down from Odysseus's home to attend.

The meeting started, and Telemachus stood up to speak. He seemed to stand taller than usual. Athena had cast a spell of pride and courage upon him. He also looked extra-handsome. Athena had done that, too.

Telemachus told the leaders of Ithaca what their sons, Penelope's suitors, were doing to his father's home. He urged them to help.

But one of the suitors interrupted Telemachus's speech. He stood up and told everyone about the tapestry Penelope seemed to be weaving.

"She promised to marry one of us when her tapestry is finished. Penelope works on her task all day long, every day. But one of her maids told me that she unravels her work every night," the suitor said, bitterly. "I am sorry, but we will not leave until she has made her choice. She must marry one of us."

"How dare you speak to me this way!" Telemachus roared. "I am the man of the house when my father is away." Athena's spell really had made him brave. "I call upon the gods to help me in my struggle. They will punish you who abuse my father's wealth and my mother's kindness." He glared at the suitors.

At that moment, two eagles appeared in midair. They were involved in a fierce battle overhead. Everyone's eyes fell on the shrieking, clawing creatures. Then the eagles flew away as quickly as they appeared.

The town's oldest and wisest man then stood up to say a few words. "You should listen to Telemachus," he warned the suitors. "Those fighting eagles are a sign. They suggest that trouble lies ahead for those who disobey. I have a very strong feeling that Odysseus will soon return. Let us be wise and put a stop to this wickedness before he comes back to Ithaca."

But most of Ithaca's leaders thought Odysseus was dead and that the eagles meant nothing. The suitors refused to leave the house, and the rest of the townsfolk refused to help.

After the meeting, Telemachus felt his

courage fading. Suddenly Athena stood before him again. She was still in her human disguise.

"You are your father's son," she reminded him. "Just like him, you are brave and strong. You will not quit or leave a job half finished. If the townspeople will not help you, you must help yourself. I will help you, too. We will find a strong ship and gather a loyal crew. We will set sail and find Odysseus. Let us not waste time. Go home and gather some supplies for the long, and possibly dangerous, voyage."

When Telemachus returned home, the suitors were in a forgiving mood. "Just give up, Telemachus," they asked. "Stop fighting us. Sit and have fun with us instead."

But Telemachus pushed past them. He did not want to hear a word they said. Downstairs, in the storage room, he found the family's faithful old nurse. He asked her to help him pack.

"But where are you going?" she asked.

"I must set sail to find my father, Odysseus," Telemachus replied. "This is the only way to make our lives better." Then he asked her for some boxes of barley meal, fragrant olive oil, and other supplies he would need for a long voyage out at sea.

The nurse began to cry. Even as she helped Telemachus gather supplies, she begged the young man not to risk his life at sea. This nurse had helped raise Odysseus, and she loved Telemachus, too. She could not bear to see him go. "The house of Odysseus," she said, "has already lost one man."

Telemachus understood her fear, but explained that he had no choice. "Now promise me that you will not tell my mother what I am planning to do," he said. "I do not want to worry her. I also do not want her to stop me from leaving." The old woman swore not to tell his secret.

At the shore, Telemachus found his ship waiting for him. It was loaded with supplies and had twenty men at the oars. Athena, still disguised as a human, stood at the rail. She held out her hand, encouraging Telemachus to board the ship.

After Telemachus stepped aboard, he and Athena took their places at the back of the ship. The goddess sent a fair wind whistling over the deep blue waves. They set off for their journey.

While Telemachus sailed, Penelope's suitors continued their bad behavior back in Ithaca. They enjoyed themselves so much that they didn't even notice Telemachus was gone.

But one day, two of the suitors overheard a sailor talking while they were in town. The sailor had just returned to Ithaca on the same ship Telemachus was using for his journey. The sailor saw the preparations for the young man's voyage. He told the two suitors that Telemachus had taken twenty men to sea in search of his father.

The two men were outraged, but secretly feared Odysseus's return. Their eyes flashed with fire as they told the news to the rest of the suitors. "We have pledged our love and given our time to waiting for the fair Penelope. We will not let some stupid boy ruin this for us."

The suitors decided that they would hire their own ship. Some of them would prepare the ship and wait in the seas around Ithaca for Telemachus to return. There, the suitors would attack him. They planned to end his life once and for all.

The loyal family nurse overheard the suitors and went upstairs to tell Penelope.

"What are you saying?" she gasped. Penelope was so upset that she had to sit down. "I didn't even know my son had left Ithaca! Now you are telling me that the suitors plan to get their own ship and try to kill him?" She began weeping loudly.

"I'm so sorry," said the dear old nurse. "I knew days ago that Telemachus had left to find Odysseus. Your son did not want you to worry and he made me promise not to tell you. Please do not cry. Try praying to Athena. She can surely save him, even from the jaws of death."

Penelope cried for a great deal longer. But eventually she did pray, and Athena heard her prayers. When Penelope fell asleep that night, Athena sent a message to her through her dreams. The goddess told Penelope that Telemachus would be fine. He was in the arms of the gods.

Penelope smiled in her sleep.

CHAPTER 3

Odysseus on Calypso's Island

⚮

Telemachus was moving along well in his journey to find Odysseus. Athena left him and his crew for a little while, not long enough for them to notice. She was restless thinking about Odysseus stuck on Calypso's island. She flew back to Mount Olympus to talk the other gods into setting him free.

"Odysseus still suffers on Calypso's island," she told her fellow gods. "Yes, she loves him and takes care of him. But Odysseus is heartsick and homesick. We must send him home," she pleaded. She also spoke of the wicked suitors' plan to attack Telemachus.

Athena's father, Zeus, hated to see his daughter unhappy. Besides, Poseidon was away, so he was unable to argue his point. Zeus decided to send Hermes, Athena's brother, to speak to Calypso. He would convince the goddess to free Odysseus.

"But, Daughter, it will not be that simple," Zeus reminded her. "Odysseus's suffering is far from over."

Hermes put on his golden sandals and flew to Calypso's island. He reached her cave. Surrounding it was a lush forest of beautiful trees. Many kinds of birds had built their nests there, and they sang wonderful songs. Grapes, violets, and all sorts of fragrant herbs bloomed under the trees. Even a god such as Hermes was charmed by the scene.

Clearly, however, one mortal was not so

charmed. Hermes saw Odysseus sitting down by the edge of the sea. He was staring sadly out over the water. Hermes knew he was thinking of home.

Hermes entered Calypso's cave. When she saw him, she recognized him at once. All the gods knew one another. She also knew exactly why he had come. Hermes did not even have to speak a word.

"You will never get me to release Odysseus!" she exclaimed. "I love him and he is mine. Zeus and the other gods must be jealous that I, a goddess, have fallen in love with a mortal man!

"And I haven't done anything wrong," she continued. "I saved Odysseus when his ship sank. I only wanted to make him immortal, so he could live with me forever."

"I come by Zeus's command," Hermes told her. "He says you must give up Odysseus."

Calypso knew she couldn't disobey Zeus.

After Hermes left, she went down to the shore to sit with Odysseus. She told him he could leave.

"I am sorry I couldn't be happy here," Odysseus said.

"It must be this way," Calypso replied. She had tears in her eyes but quickly wiped them away. "Go cut some beams of wood and make yourself a sturdy raft. I will put bread and water on board, so you won't starve. I will also give you clothes to keep you warm, and a fair wind to take you home. It is settled."

But Odysseus was nervous. "Goddess," he said. "Do you really mean to help me? You cannot truly want me to sail this rough sea on just a raft, no matter how sturdy it is. Please promise me that this is not a trick of some kind."

Calypso took his hand. "Your trip will not be easy," she admitted. "But this is what the gods have decided. This raft is your only way off my island. Go back to your life in Ithaca. Go back to your wife. The heavens above and earth below are my witnesses. I promise I am not trying to trick or hurt you. My heart is not made of iron. I do love you, and I am very sorry for you."

With these words, Odysseus followed Calypso to the cave. He sat and ate a final meal with her.

"Are you sure you don't want to stay here with me?" she asked him. "Surely, your wife is not taller or more beautiful than I am?"

"Calypso," Odysseus said. "You are a goddess. Of course no mortal woman could compare. But I love my wife more than anything."

Calypso nodded, and the two of them went to sleep. When morning came, Odysseus was ready to build his raft. Calypso handed him a beautiful ax with an olive-wood handle. She led him to the far end of the island, where the driest and best trees could be found. He would make his raft out of these.

Odysseus quickly cut down twenty trees. He

chopped them into planks of wood for the raft. In no time, he had tied all the wood together and fitted the raft with a mast and a wheel. Calypso gave Odysseus some linen to make his sails. Together they pulled the raft into the water. It was time for Odysseus to set sail for home.

Pushed by Calypso's fair wind, Odysseus sailed for seventeen days without seeing land. Finally, he could see the outlines of the Phaeacian coast on the horizon.

But Poseidon, the mighty god of the sea, was flying overhead. He caught sight of Odysseus down below. The sea god was furious that his fellow gods had decided to help Odysseus. Poseidon gathered the clouds together and stirred up the sea. He called forth the anger of every earthly wind. The sea and sky darkened. Both were hidden by thick black clouds.

Odysseus's heart began to beat faster. The sea got rougher. A giant wave broke over his tiny raft with force and fury. Odysseus was thrown overboard. He stayed underwater for a long time, unable to breathe. Gathering all his energy, Odysseus swam back to the surface. He spotted the raft, swam toward it, and climbed back on. Again, the sea crashed against the raft. Thunder boomed. Odysseus could feel the sea god's rage. Then Poseidon sent one final wave, twenty-five feet tall. The force of it destroyed Odysseus's tiny raft. Odysseus plunged back into the sea.

But Athena was watching. She knew she had to save Odysseus from the anger of Poseidon. With all her might she held back the forceful winds, except for one. That one wind was stronger than the rest. It sent Odysseus toward the land of the Phaeacians. Athena knew he would be safe once he arrived there.

For two days and two nights, Odysseus floated and tossed upon the sea. On the morning of the third day, he finally saw the Phaeacian coastline once more. It was sharp and rocky. Odysseus could have been thrown against the rocks by the waves. He could have been hurt. But Athena guided him safely in to shore. She led him toward the mouth of a river.

Odysseus was exhausted. After floating down the river for a while, he pulled himself up onto the bank. Odysseus was so happy to be back on dry land that he fell down among the grasses and kissed the ground. Odysseus also thanked Athena, whom he sensed was there helping him.

The bruised and beaten Odysseus sat there for a time. Then he went to search for a better place to rest. He found some leafy trees higher up over the river's edge. It was a nice, hidden place to have some peace and quiet. Odysseus gathered a pile of leaves to lie on. Athena cast a spell of sweet sleep over him. She made him lose all memory of his sorrows and struggles. Odysseus happily closed his eyes.

While Odysseus slept, Athena went inland to look around. It was important that this was a place where Odysseus could be safe. She arrived at the city of the Phaeacians and found the castle of their ruler, King Alcinous.

Athena made herself invisible and slipped straight into the bedroom of the king's daughter. While the princess slept, Athena put an idea into her head: The next day, she should go with some friends down to the river and wash the family's clothes.

In the morning, the princess woke with a sudden urge to go to the river. She gathered friends, asked her father for a horse and wagon, and took the group to the river. She brought the family's clothes to be washed.

The girls washed the clothes and hung them to dry. After the chore was done, they went swimming. They played joyfully, giggling and calling out to one another.

Their laughing and shouting woke up Odysseus, who was sleeping close by. He rose, stretched, and crept out from behind the trees. Odysseus covered himself with leafy branches because most of his clothes had been torn to shreds in the ocean. When the girls saw the strange man, they screamed. They all ran away except for the princess. Athena had put courage into her heart.

"Please do not be afraid," Odysseus said. "I need your help. I have sailed here on a tiny raft. The winds and waves flung me about and I almost drowned. But a favorable wind brought me here. You are the first person I've met on this island. I beg you—can you please lend me some of your clothes and show me to town?"

The princess looked at the man carefully. His face looked sensible and polite. Besides, she was not alone. Her friends had slowly returned one by one, no longer afraid of him. The girls now gathered around him, offering safety and friendship.

"I am the king's daughter, and our people are called the Phaeacians," the princess said. "It is our nature to be helpful to travelers. I will give you some clothes and show you the way to town."

Odysseus was overjoyed. The Phaeacians were known throughout the land as kind and generous people. They had lived up to this reputation.

But the princess also had some rules. They would bring Odysseus back in their wagon, but they would leave him at the city's outer wall. He would have to come into town on his own.

"It would not be proper," the princess said, "if I—a young woman and princess—entered town with a strange man." She didn't want to be a subject for the town's gossips. Odysseus agreed to this. They arrived at the city's outer walls, and Odysseus got out of the wagon.

The princess pointed out a patch of trees by the road. This was where Odysseus would wait. "Then come to the palace by yourself and ask for my mother, the queen," she instructed.

"Not your father, the king?" Odysseus asked.

"My mother is the one you need to win over," the princess said, smiling.

CHAPTER 4

Odysseus Arrives at the Palace

The princess returned to the palace with the laundry. She acted as if everything were normal, going up to her room without a word. Meanwhile, Odysseus waited in the trees outside town, just as the princess had instructed.

Athena suddenly appeared by his side. Odysseus was happy to see the goddess who had helped him survive Poseidon's storm. She offered him some advice. "When you go in," she said, "do not be afraid. The more confident you act, the more likely you are to be trusted."

Odysseus thanked her and made his way to the king's palace. Outside, the palace garden was full of beautiful trees. Luscious pears, pomegranates, apples, figs, and olives hung from the branches. A stream ran through the garden, watering colorful beds of flowers.

The palace walls were made of bronze, with a trim of royal-blue tiles. The golden doors were framed by silver. Odysseus was stunned at the beauty of this Phaeacian palace. All around the inner courtyard, people were working. Some servants were grinding rich, yellow grain. Others worked at looms, weaving tapestries and rugs. People carried things back and forth. All was lively and active.

But when Odysseus arrived, everyone stopped their activity and watched. They were shocked as this stranger walked straight up to the queen and kneeled before her.

"O Queen," Odysseus exclaimed, "I understand you are the woman to talk to. I humbly ask Your Majesty—please help me return to my own country. I have been at sea and away from my family for too long."

The ruler, Queen Arete, welcomed him, as the Phaeacians were always kind to travelers. This stranger seemed brave and gentle. The queen had a good feeling about him. She introduced him to her husband, King Alcinous. They invited the stranger to join them for supper.

Odysseus sat down at their grand table. A fine meal was set in front of them, and it smelled delicious. Odysseus realized it had been a long time since anyone had invited him to dine. They began to eat. The king and queen made polite conversation with their guest.

At once, Queen Arete recognized the shirt and cloak Odysseus was wearing. It was her own design. She had sewn these clothes for her sons.

"Where did you get your clothes?" she asked.

Instead of giving the short answer, Odysseus told her his whole story. He spoke about how he had been held captive by Calypso, then set free. How he had sailed from the island in a tiny raft, and braved the mighty anger of Poseidon. How he arrived at Phaeacia and how her kind daughter had helped him.

The king and queen were amazed by his story. They agreed that this man had been on quite an adventure! After supper, the queen showed him to his guest room. Everyone in the palace went to bed. As Odysseus fell asleep, he thanked Athena for bringing him to this place.

The next day, the king invited his trusted counselors to a meeting. He wanted to discuss their guest.

"Hear me, hear me," he said, standing before his loyal men. "This stranger needs our generosity and kindness." He placed his hand on Odysseus's shoulder. "The reputation of our people is that we are kind to travelers. Let us work together to build him a fine ship. Fifty of our finest young men shall volunteer to be his crew. We will escort him safely back home."

Odysseus was thrilled to hear this. Everyone knew the Phaeacians were also masters of the sea. In fact, it was said their ships didn't even need captains or wheels. As if by magic, their boats knew where the captain wanted to go. These ships could sail safely even when the sea was covered in mist and clouds. They could go on even when others had to stop. On a Phaeacian boat, there was no danger. That is how it had always been.

It would take only a few days to prepare Odysseus's boat. In the meantime, the king invited the kingdom to the palace for a festival. The ballroom was set up with rows and rows of long tables. Odysseus was invited again to feast beside the king and queen. They had a special table at the head of the room. Again, there was plenty of delicious food set before them.

For entertainment, the king had hired a famous singer. As the guests ate and drank, the singer performed a song about the Trojan War. Nobody knew their guest of honor was Odysseus, the great warrior who had experienced the war and its many sad battles.

Odysseus tried hard to mask his feelings. But his emotions overwhelmed him during the sad song. The king noticed his guest was upset.

"Enough singing!" the king said. "In addition to our kindness to strangers, Phaeacians are known for our athletic skill. I want our guest to tell his countrymen how talented we are as boxers, wrestlers, jumpers, and runners. Let the games begin!"

Quickly the crowds gathered to show off their talents. First were the footraces. Then some of the strongest men competed in disk throwing and boxing. The king's son was the best boxer. The young man noticed that Odysseus was just sitting there, watching.

"Sir, you seem very fit," he said. "How about joining us in some sport?"

"Thank you, but my mind is too focused on going home to think about games," Odysseus answered.

Another young man rolled his eyes. "Excuses, excuses," he said. "I guess you are not the athlete we thought you might be."

Odysseus became annoyed. "And so what if I am not?" he asked. "Not all men are athletes. Some are good speakers. Others are handsome, but foolish. I have other things on my mind. The sea and my suffering have made me tired and weak. But you have made me mad and deserve to be put in your place."

Odysseus turned and picked up a disk. It was

much heavier than any other. He threw it much farther than any Phaeacian had thrown a disk.

"What's next?" he asked, looking back at his challenger. "I will compete with any man, in any sport!"

But the wise King Alcinous thought it best to end the competition. He changed the subject yet again. "Why don't you tell us your name instead?" he asked.

He took a deep breath and told the king who he was. "I am Odysseus, king of Ithaca. I have been traveling since the end of the Trojan War, trying to get back to my home." The crowd gasped—they couldn't believe it was Odysseus! Their voices rose to an uproar.

King Alcinous had to quiet the crowd. He shouted, "Silence! Order!" The crowd hushed. The king continued. "Dear Odysseus, we are honored to have you in our kingdom. Perhaps you can tell us a story of your travels."

Odysseus smiled. "Just one story?" he asked. After all, he had so many. "In my long journey home to Ithaca, I have encountered many things. I have faced many dangers, troubles, and struggles. My tale is long and winding, but I will tell it since you have asked."

And then he began the tale of his journey.

CHAPTER 5

Odysseus Begins His Tale

⌒

THE CICONES

"When I first set off from Troy, after the war, the wind first took me to Ismarus, home of the Cicones. During the war, those people were on the side of the Trojans, our enemies. So my men and I decided to take over the seaside city. We destroyed much of it, and gathered many of its treasures. At that point, I wanted to leave, but my men were foolish and greedy. They wanted to stay longer and take even more.

"We did not know that the Cicones had

sent a message to their brothers who lived farther inland. There were many more of them. They were organized and skilled warriors who surprised us with a counterattack. Although we fought bravely, they were able to defeat us. They killed many of my men and drove us away from their land. When we finally got back to our ships to sail away, each crew was missing six men."

THE LOTUS EATERS

"One day at sea, a great storm came down upon our ship. My men and I were driven off course. Our ship landed on a beautiful, tropical island where people lived by eating lotus flowers," Odysseus said.

"Some of my men went ashore and sampled the flower. It was said to taste like the most delicate honey—like the nectar the gods drank. It was so delicious that they wandered off and forgot all about home. As if under a magical spell, they wanted to stay on the island forever, munching lazily on lotus flowers. Oh, how frustrated I was with them! After all, we were on a journey, and we had not reached the end. How they wept when I forced them back to our ship! But I closed my ears and heart to their protests. I was determined to return to my home."

THE KING OF THE CYCLOPES

"Sailing through the dark and foggy night, we spotted a coastline," Odysseus said. "Once we anchored we recognized the land as the home of the Cyclopes. These are giant, wild creatures who have only one eye in the middle of their heads. They have no laws and are quite savage. They live in caves. We had heard that these creatures did not own ships or know how to sail. We felt safe a good distance off their shore.

"The next morning, we decided to explore the island. We wanted to see what the Cyclopes were like. At what other time would we have the chance? Just to be safe, we brought a jug of water mixed with a magic sleeping potion. We thought this might help us out of any problems.

"When we got to the island, we found a large cave where many sheep and goats were being kept. We figured it must be the home of a Cyclops. In the cave were shelves full of delicious cheeses and crates full of milk. My men and I were hungry and curious. We decided to explore the cave, but quickly.

"But then the Cyclops returned from gathering his sheep. He was enormous and awful. My men and I were frightened for our lives. We hid at the far end of the cave in the dark. The Cyclops couldn't see us there. He called the rest of his sheep inside, then rolled a boulder over the mouth of the cave. We were trapped inside

with the great beast! The boulder was so large that even two dozen horse-drawn wagons could not have removed it. We feared for our lives.

"Then the Cyclops turned around and saw us! He asked, 'Strangers, who are you? Where do you sail from?' We told him we had been driven off course by the weather. We asked kindly for his friendship. But without another word, the monster picked up two of my men and ate them up! Then he went to sleep.

"As you might imagine," Odysseus continued, "I was beyond angry. I wanted to kill the Cyclops right there in his sleep to get revenge. But I knew we could not move that boulder from the cave's entrance without his help. We waited until morning, and tried to remain calm. I paced around the cave all night, trying to calm myself.

"Morning came. The monster woke, lit his fire, then ate two more of my men for breakfast. Then he rolled away the boulder to let his sheep out. Before my men and I could escape, he rolled the boulder back into its place."

"What did you do then?" asked King Alcinous. He was sitting on the edge of his chair in suspense.

"I came up with a plan," Odysseus replied. "I found a large branch near one of the sheep pens. I ordered my men to work together to sharpen and burn one end. Then we hid our spear and waited for the monster's return.

"That night, the Cyclops came back to the cave. Again he rolled the boulder back into place behind him. After he milked his sheep, he ate two more of my men for supper. I was in a rage! But I kept calm. I brought the beast a bowl of the water mixed with sleeping potion.

"'Look here,' I said. 'We brought you this special drink as a gift. Will you please take it and stop eating my men?'

"The greedy monster drank. He was so

delighted with our gift that he asked for another bowlful, then another. 'Tell me your name,' the Cyclops said. 'You can trust me. I want to give you a gift, too.'

"I could see that the potion had made the monster weak and weary," said Odysseus. "But I still did not trust him. So I told him my name was Noman.

"The Cyclops laughed. 'Then I will eat all of Noman's friends and keep Noman for dessert!' the monster roared. 'That is the gift I will give him!' With that, the monster fell to the ground and began snoring.

"'Now!' I cried. My men grabbed the spear from its hiding place. We heated it in the fire until it was glowing hot. Then we drove it into the beast's one terrible eye, blinding him.

"The beast's screams echoed throughout the cave. He ran around in a frenzy, calling out to all the other Cyclopes on the island for help.

"'Polyphemus,' they called, for that was the beast's name. 'Are you all right? Why are you shouting? Surely no man is trying to kill you by trickery or force?'

"'Yes!' the Cyclops shouted back. 'Noman is killing me by trickery! Noman is killing me by force!' But his friends thought '*no* man' was attacking the Cyclops. They went back home and the beast collapsed to the ground. Exhausted from our battle, he fell asleep.

"Still, we were trapped in the cave. I had to figure a way to get us out. The next morning, the Cyclops moved the boulder to let his sheep out. It took him much longer now that he was blind. I saw the monster put his hands out, feeling the fur of every sheep as they went through the cave's entrance. He wanted to make sure they were animals, not us men.

"This action sparked my mind. At that moment, I came up with a plan. My men and

I tied ourselves to the fluffy bellies of the biggest sheep. It was tough to ride on the underside of the animals, but it worked. When we arrived at the door of the cave, all the Cyclops could feel was fluff and fur. We had escaped!

"Well, almost," Odysseus added, embarrassed. "We had sailed a safe distance away. I was still so angry at the Cyclops for eating some of my finest men. I stood up and shouted back toward the land. I told him he got what he deserved.

"The Cyclops became furious. He tore the top off of a mountain and flung it at my ship. The sea rose so much that the wave carried us back to shore.

"We rowed for our lives and escaped again. But I wasn't finished. My men begged me not to speak another word, but my anger got the best of me. I shouted out again, 'Cyclops, if anyone asks you who blinded you, it was not Noman. It was *this* man, the brave warrior Odysseus, from Ithaca!'

"This," Odysseus finished sadly, "was a mistake. You see, the Cyclops's father is Poseidon, the sea god. The gods can hear everything, so he immediately knew it was I who had blinded his son. Since that day I have been cursed. Poseidon does not want me to live for what I have done to his son. He has caused me great suffering."

CHAPTER 6

Odysseus Continues His Tale

~oo~

THE MAGICAL BAG OF WINDS

"Soon we reached a peaceful island that floated on top of the sea. The island's elder, Aeolus, was a generous host. He let us rest, and gave us food and water. I told him our sad tale of roaming the seas on our way back home. He felt pity for us and wanted to help. Aeolus presented me with a magical sack made of leather. He told me he had captured the roaring winds and tied them up in the sack. Zeus had made him captain of the winds. He could stir or still each of them when he wanted.

"Before he gave me the sack, he tied it so tightly. Not even a tiny puff of air could escape. He only allowed the fair West Wind to blow. It was to take us home smoothly. Aeolus told me to keep it safe and near me at all times. I was not to tell my crew what was in the bag. I agreed, and we sailed on our way.

"We sailed for ten days. I kept my eye on that bag of winds the whole time. It was exhausting, but I didn't want to take any chances. Soon we came so close to Ithaca that we could see the smoke rising from our own chimneys. I finally relaxed and closed my eyes for a minute.

"This was another mistake. As soon as I had begun to sleep, my men let their curiosity about the sack take over. One of them took it from my side. He thought it contained treasure that I was hiding from the crew. He tore open the sack, and the winds rushed out. This great mistake caused a terrible storm. The winds thrashed about, howling in our ears. They carried us, weeping terribly, back out to sea. All the way back, in fact, to the island we had come from.

"Aeolus was shocked when we returned. 'What happened?' he asked. 'I took great pains to get you home.'

"I told him my men, and cruel sleep, had ruined me. I begged him to give us another bag of winds, but he refused. 'Clearly you are cursed by the gods,' he said.

"We moved on, without his help."

THE GODDESS CIRCE

"Next I will tell you about the goddess Circe— now, this is quite a tale!" Odysseus said. "We finally arrived at another island and anchored nearby. My crew and I were terribly worn out. Our bodies and minds were tired. After getting a good night's sleep on the ship, I sent half of my men to shore. I asked them to come back and report what they saw.

"They found a small stone house. Fierce wolves and mountain lions prowled around the outside. But instead of attacking my men, the animals wagged their tails as if they were friendly puppies. The creatures rubbed their noses lovingly against the sailors. It seemed that someone had tamed them with magic.

"When they knocked on the door of the goddess Circe, she welcomed the men. All trusted and followed her—all except for my first mate, who was leading the mission. He suspected trouble.

"He was right. Circe fed the men a great feast of cheese, honey, bread, and olives. But she had dropped a sleeping potion onto the food.

When my men became sleepy, she used her magic to turn them into pigs! She locked them up in a pen and ignored their squealing.

"My first mate was the only one who didn't eat. He ran back to the ship to tell me what had happened. He was too afraid to return, so I went. As I entered the forest surrounding Circe's house, I met Hermes with his golden wand. He was in the form of a young man.

"He gave me a special herb—a black root with a white flower. If I ate the herb, it would protect me from Circe's spells. Hermes also told me how to respond when she tried to charm me.

"'When she waves her magic wand at you,' he said, 'draw your sword and spring forward. Pretend you are going to kill her. She will be frightened but will respect you. She will ask you to stay and be her companion. You must not refuse her, for you want her to set your men free. But you must make her promise that she will not cause any more trouble.'

"And so I ate the herb and went to Circe's house," Odysseus continued. "When I knocked on Circe's door, she let me in. She gave me a goblet of drink. I knew it was poisoned, but I drank it anyway. The herb would protect me.

"Then she waved her wand. She may have been trying to turn me into a pig. I rushed at her with my sword. She screamed, fell to the ground, and clasped my knees.

"'Who and what are you?' she asked, amazed. 'How can it be that my magic has no power over you? You are spell-proof. Surely, you must be none other than the bold hero Odysseus. Hermes always said you would come here. You and I would make a fine match.'

"I demanded that she promise never to harm me or my men. At first she hesitated, because gods must always keep their promises. But then she agreed.

"Circe brought my men into the room. They were still squealing, muddy pigs. The goddess walked among the pigs and dropped a magical potion on them, one by one. They turned back into my men. The men were even younger and better looking than they had been before."

"And then you left?" King Alcinous asked Odysseus.

"Well, no," he admitted. "Perhaps I was not as protected from Circe's magic as I thought. She charmed me. I stayed with her for a whole year. I forgot all about home, until one of my men reminded me. Then I quickly remembered and made plans to leave Circe at once."

"And then you left for home?" Queen Arete asked.

"No," Odysseus said. "Circe told me I first had to go to Hades, the underworld where the dead live. The way to get there was to sail the River Styx. There I was to make offerings to the gods. Also, I was to seek advice from the ghost of the blind prophet Teiresias. He would be able to tell me how to get home.

"Circe told me that we would not need a guide. We only needed to raise our mast, set our sails, and the North Wind would blow us to the River Styx. This would take us to Hades.

"Of course my men were upset and frightened. They did not want to go to Hades. It is where most men go only after they die. No mortal man should go there."

CHAPTER 7

The Living Visit the Dead

~⚬~

"My men were quiet and serious as we boarded our ship," Odysseus said. "Circe, that great and clever goddess, sent us a fair wind. We reached the River Styx with no problems. We were at the edge of Hades by nightfall. It was the entrance to a frightful place where no living men were meant to go.

"Almost as soon as we arrived, the ghosts came. Young brides and bachelors, old men worn out from work, brave men and fellow soldiers who had been lost in battle, and many more. My men were shaking and covering their eyes. Some of them were crying. They did not want to visit with the dead. Neither did I. But it was part of our journey. We pushed on.

"We began to arrange some gifts we had brought for the spirits. The ghosts tried to grab our gifts, but I would not let them. I needed some answers first.

"One of the first ghosts who came close to us was Agamemnon, my old friend from the Trojan War," Odysseus said. "He told me that when he returned to Sparta after the war, his wife had married another man. She and her new husband had killed him upon his return.

"I was devastated to hear of my friend's sad end. Agamemnon warned me that I could not trust my wife, Penelope. His advice was not to tell anyone I was coming home. He suggested I show up suddenly, unannounced, to see if she has been true to me.

"Next appeared the ghost I had especially come to see, the prophet Teiresias. He carried a golden staff in his hand. I asked him when and how we could get back to Ithaca. Teiresias told me our trip home would be hard. Poseidon still felt much bitterness toward me for blinding his son. The sea god was trying to make my journey difficult.

"Teiresias then mentioned that we would need to travel past the island of the Sun God. We would still get home if we could behave ourselves while we were there. It was important that we leave his beautiful flocks of sheep and cattle alone. If we could do that, the rest of our trip home would be smooth. We just had to make sure we didn't touch the Sun God's animals.

"Teiresias knew many things about me. He also told me about Penelope's suitors at my home in Ithaca. When he said this, my face became hot

and anger filled my body. Teiresias noticed, and told me I would get my revenge."

Odysseus bowed his head. This next part of the story was hard to tell. "After I spoke with Teiresias," he said, "the ghosts came out to greet us. A parade of all the people I had known passed in front of me. Each of my men experienced the same thing. The ghosts of their friends, family, and foes swirled around each of them, wanting to speak. For me, the brave soldiers who fought and died beside me in Troy came to shake my hand. Of course I could not grip them since they were ghosts.

"It was hardest for me to see my dear mother, who was alive when I left Ithaca for battle. I never got to say my last good-byes to her. She told me that she had died of sadness waiting for me to come home to Ithaca. I was heartbroken, and tried to hug her. But of course, she was a ghost. So my arms passed right through her. It was like hugging the air.

"Some of the ghosts were being punished for the wrongs they had committed during their lives," Odysseus said, trembling. "It was horrible to watch. The ghost of a man named Tantalus stood in a beautiful freshwater lake.

Above his head hung branches full of fruits—pears, pomegranates, apples, sweet figs, and juicy olives. Yet Tantalus will be hungry and thirsty forever. For each time he reached up to grab the fruits, the wind tossed them out of his grasp. And whenever he bent down to take a drink, the water dropped out of his reach.

"And I saw another ghost," Odysseus added, "named Sisyphus. His punishment was to roll a big stone up to the top of a hill. Whenever he was almost at the top, the stone would slip from his hands and roll back down the mountain. This happened over and over again. I saw the look of failure in his eyes.

"After a while," Odysseus concluded, "I couldn't take any more. I had to get out of Hades. No wonder most mortals are not allowed to go there. I bid Teiresias farewell and thanked him for his wise advice. My men and I then gladly came back up to the world of the living."

CHAPTER 8

Odysseus Finishes His Tale

෴

And Odysseus had even more stories to tell the king and queen of Phaeacia!

THE SIRENS

"At last, we were clear of the River Styx and back onto the open sea," Odysseus continued. "My men and I could finally relax, now that we were out of the underworld. Each of us had been changed by that visit. No one spoke another word of the horrific Hades.

"After sailing for a few days, we came close to the island of the Sirens. The Sirens are magical singers. They enchant all who come near enough to hear them. Anyone who hears their song is drawn to their island and is never able to leave. Sirens' songs are irresistible. Listeners forget about home, family, and even food. They become wrapped in the melody and eventually waste away.

"Circe had warned me about the Sirens. She advised me to fill my men's ears with wax. That way they'd never be able to hear the Sirens' songs. She suggested, though, that I listen in order to experience the rare pleasure. But first I must get my men to tie me to the ship's mast, she said. As we approached the island of the Sirens, my men tied me to the mast with the strongest knots. I made them promise not to untie me, no matter how I begged."

"And did you beg?" asked Queen Arete.

Odysseus confessed that, after hearing the Sirens' song, he did. "For their voices were unlike any other in the world. They sang my past and future. They sang my fortunes and misfortunes. They sang my soul and mind all in the same tune. All temptation came from their throats.

"I begged for my life to be let go. All I could think of was the island of the Sirens. I thought I would go mad as I was bound in those tight knots. But my men were trustworthy. They only made the ropes tighter. They quickened their rowing. Soon we were past the island and my mind quieted."

SCYLLA AND CHARYBDIS

"After the Sirens," he continued, "we had to sail through a passage guarded by two monsters, Scylla and Charybdis. Each monster sat at one edge of the passage. We had to decide which side to take.

"We decided to take the side guarded by the monster Scylla. She had twelve feet and six necks! At the end of each neck she had a horrible head, each with three rows of teeth. She crunched men to death. As our ship sailed through, Scylla clawed and snapped at us. We were terrified, but Charybdis would have been a worse monster to pass.

"Charybdis sat on the other side of the passage. She sucked the seawater all the way in, creating a whirlpool. Then she spit all the water back up, creating a giant wave. But Circe had advised us to pass on the Scylla side, so we did.

"Scylla pounced on us with all of her horrible heads. She snatched up six of my best men, which threw me into another rage. I had to contain my anger to save my other men. We managed to fight her off long enough to pass by her.

"With that trouble behind us, we continued on. I knew my men needed to rest. So did I. We looked for a calm island where we could stay to refresh ourselves."

THE ISLAND OF THE SUN GOD

"Eventually we came to the island of the Sun God. This was the one Teiresias had told us about. The Sun God's very special sheep and cattle would be tempting. But these were the animals we had been warned not to touch."

Odysseus explained that he and his men anchored at the island. They rested comfortably for a few days. With enough supplies to feed the crew, they left the sheep and cattle alone.

But soon they ran out of food. The men had even eaten all the fish from the sea. They were starving. The sheep and cattle were starting to tempt them.

"But I warned them still not to touch the animals," Odysseus explained. "One day, I had gone inland in search of other food. My men could not stand their hunger any longer. They gave in. While I was gone, the men stole one of the cows. They put together a fire and threw themselves a feast.

"I could smell the delicious roast meat as I got closer to our ship. I prayed, 'Please don't let that be what I think it is!' But of course, it was. My men had stolen and eaten one of the Sun God's cows. I began to scold them for disobeying.

"But then the Sun God flew into a rage. His voice boomed overhead, cursing us in the name of all the gods. The Sun God threatened to stop shining upon the earth unless we were punished.

"We fled the island. As soon as we were back out to sea, Zeus shot a lightning bolt at us. It destroyed the ship and sent us plunging to our deaths in the rough sea.

"All of my men drowned. I was the only survivor." The great hero Odysseus said this slowly and sadly. The king and queen could tell that he missed his men terribly. More than that, Odysseus felt he had failed. None of his brave crew would ever see their homes again.

After the shipwreck, Odysseus explained, he had drifted through the sea on a plank of wood. Somehow he arrived back at the terrible whirlpool of Charybdis. Odysseus got sucked down. The seas swirled around his head like a violent, dangerous funnel.

"At last, Charybdis spit out the water and let me go," Odysseus finished. "I climbed back onto my plank of wood and began to paddle. I drifted for ten days until I reached Calpyso's island. I remained there for ten years. This was the place I left before I sailed here on my raft.

"You have all been so kind to this worn-out, weary man. The Phaeacians have truly proven to be a generous people. And now I have told you the whole story of my sad and winding journey."

CHAPTER 9

The Phaeacians Send Odysseus Home

The king, the queen, and the rest of the court clapped after Odysseus finished his stories. It was hard to believe he had been through so much and survived. Odysseus was indeed as brave and strong as legend said he was.

"Odysseus," said the king, "I think we all agree that you have been through enough. Soon you will leave Phaeacia to sail to Ithaca. You will take many gifts with you."

The evening before Odysseus was to sail

away, the king held a farewell banquet in the hero's honor. Even as he ate with the kind Phaeacians, Odysseus looked toward the sun. He wanted to speed its setting. He longed to be on his way home.

In the morning, Odysseus and his Phaeacian crew boarded a great ship. Once it set sail, the ship bounded forward like an eager racehorse. The front curved like the neck of a beautiful stallion. The ship left a great wave of dark blue water in its wake as it moved gracefully and smoothly over the sea. The Phaeacians proudly sailed the ship toward Ithaca, Odysseus's home. Odysseus slept soundly the whole way, dreaming of Penelope and Telemachus.

When they reached the Ithacan shore, the Phaeacians did not wake Odysseus. They gently lifted him off the ship and laid him down under an olive tree. Odysseus would be hidden there until he woke up. The men arranged all the king's gifts on the ground around Odysseus. Then they left to sail back home.

Poseidon saw the Phaeacian ship leaving Ithaca. The sea god knew it had brought Odysseus home. Poseidon felt the Phaeacians had disrespected him by helping Odysseus.

He followed the ship back to Phaeacia. Just as it sailed into harbor, Poseidon turned the whole ship into stone. It then plunged to the bottom of the sea. The sea god wanted to teach the Phaeacians a lesson about disrespecting the gods. In fact, he did. The Phaeacian people saw it all happen. They never again showed kindness to any stranger passing through their land.

When Odysseus woke, he didn't know where he was. He had been away for so long that he didn't even know his own home. Just as he always did when arriving somewhere new, he wondered, *What will the people of this place be like?*

He looked around at the gifts the Phaeacians had given him. There were gold goblets, well-crafted jugs, and beautiful blankets. He searched for someplace to hide his treasure. At that moment, Athena came to him. She was disguised as a young shepherd.

"My friend," said Odysseus, "you are the first person I have met in this new country. Can you tell me where I am?"

The shepherd told him he was in Ithaca. Odysseus was used to lying to strangers about who he really was. He automatically said, "Oh, yes! Ithaca—I have heard of that place."

Athena smiled and turned back into her goddess form. She joked with him. "Odysseus," she asked, "won't you ever stop your tricks? You do not have to lie to protect yourself. It is me, Athena! I have been keeping watch over you during your journey."

"You are one to speak about lying," he teased

her back. "You are always in disguises! And where were you before I reached the Phaeacians? Where were you when I was suffering? Is this some kind of trick now? Or am I finally back in Ithaca?"

"I am very sorry for your suffering," Athena said. "I did not want to anger Poseidon. He still wants revenge upon you for blinding his son. But let me make it up to you now." Athena helped Odysseus finish hiding the Phaeacians' gifts.

"Now," Athena went on, "I will help you come up with a plan for you to return home. I will help you face those wicked suitors."

First, they decided, Odysseus was to tell no one else his true identity. No one should know he had returned to Ithaca. To make this easier, Athena disguised Odysseus as an old beggar man. She covered his body with wrinkles. She made his blond hair disappear so he looked bald. Athena turned his clothes to rags, then sent him to his own home.

When he got there, he was to speak to his loyal old swineherd. This man lived in a small house on Odysseus's property.

In the meantime, Athena would go to Sparta to see Telemachus. It was time for him to stop searching for his father and come home.

"My family doesn't know I am alive," Odysseus suddenly realized. "I cannot wait to see my wife and son. Please, Athena, bring me to them now!"

"No, you must stay in disguise until I tell you to reveal your true identity," Athena explained. "This is the way it must be." With that, she left.

Odysseus hiked until he reached the edge of his property. There he saw his old loyal swineherd, named Eumaeus. Odysseus noticed there were fewer pigs than there used to be. But he could see that Eumaeus had been taking good care of his animals and land.

When Eumaeus's dogs saw Odysseus, they started to bark. The dogs ran toward him, wagging their tails. Eumaeus called them off.

"Old man, you should not wander onto other people's property," he told Odysseus. "Those dogs might have made a meal of you. I don't need any more problems. Already I have lost my wonderful master. Now I have to tend pigs for some greedy suitors to eat."

Eumaeus invited Odysseus, still disguised as a beggar, inside. He saw that the beggar needed to eat and rest. Odysseus sat down where Eumaeus told him to and ate what was brought to him. The master was pleased by his servant's generosity to strangers. Eumaeus then told him about the suitors who had occupied Odysseus's home.

"These suitors are trying to marry fair Penelope, wife of my beloved master," Eumaeus said. "It sickens me. We do not even know if Odysseus is dead or alive!"

When he was done eating and drinking, Odysseus said, "My friend, do not worry about your master. Do not be concerned that the greedy suitors will succeed. I promise you, Odysseus is coming back. He will get his revenge."

Eumaeus sighed. "I hope you are right," he said.

Because he could not help it, Odysseus tested the swineherd's loyalty.

"I do not want to trouble you anymore," he said. "Tomorrow I will go begging in the city. Perhaps someone else will give me a drink and a piece of bread. I will go to Odysseus's house and ask the suitors if they will give me dinner."

The swineherd was bothered by this idea. "You must stay far away from those horrible suitors!" he exclaimed. "They would not be kind to you. Once Telemachus comes home, he will give you a shirt and cloak. We will send you wherever you want to go. But you must stay here with me in the meantime."

Still, Odysseus tested him. "Please, Eumaeus," he said. "The wind has picked up and a cold rain has begun. Can't *you* give me a cloak?"

Although he had none extra, Eumaeus gave Odysseus the cloak off his own back. Odysseus wrapped himself in it. Then he lay down and fell asleep in front of the fire. His old friend was more loyal and true than Odysseus could have ever imagined.

∾

Athena had already arrived in Sparta. She found Telemachus and approached him.

"Telemachus," Athena said. "You did a brave thing. Not all young men would set out to search for their fathers. Now it is time for you to go home. Your mother needs you." She explained that one of the suitors was trying too hard to convince Penelope to marry him. He kept bothering her even when Penelope told him to leave her alone. Telemachus said he would leave as soon as possible.

"Wait," Athena said. "There is one more thing. Some of the suitors are waiting for you in Ithaca's harbor. They mean to kill you before you reach home. Steer your ship to the other side of the island. Anchor there instead. You will have a longer hike back to your house, but you will be safe."

Athena also asked him to go straight to the house of Eumaeus to spend the night. The following day, he could go back home and let his mother know he was all right. Telemachus agreed.

Back on his ship, Telemachus ordered his men to lift the sails. They loosened the ropes holding the ship to the dock. Athena sent them a fair, strong wind. The ship sailed back to Ithaca as quickly as possible.

CHAPTER 10

Odysseus and Telemachus Meet Again

Telemachus arrived back in Ithaca safely thanks to Athena's advice. He sent his crew back to town. As Athena had ordered, Telemachus went to visit the swineherd, Eumaeus.

Eumaeus's dogs spotted Telemachus. The dogs ran to him, yipping happily as if they were puppies. They remembered the young Telemachus.

Eumaeus saw his young master and kissed his forehead. He wept for joy. It was as if Telemachus were his own son returning from a long journey.

"Tell me, old friend," Telemachus asked quickly. "How is my mother?"

"She is still at the house," replied Eumaeus. "She still cries day and night over your father."

Telemachus entered the house. Odysseus, still in disguise, rose to give the young man his seat. Telemachus stopped him. "Sit down, stranger," he said, politely. "I can sit on the floor."

Odysseus was proud of his handsome son. He was pleased with the way his son treated a poor stranger. Telemachus sat on the floor. The three men had breakfast together.

"Stranger," Telemachus said to Odysseus, "I would like to take you to my home. I will give you some good clothes, sandals, and a sword. My mother and I will certainly feed you a good meal. I am still young and could fight back if the suitors attacked me. But I could not protect you, if the suitors were to attack you."

Odysseus listened patiently. "If I were

young," he told his son gently, "and the son of the noble Odysseus, I would show my strength. You should march straight to your home and make those suitors regret they ever entered it!"

Telemachus nodded, moved by the stranger's words. He asked Eumaeus to go to Penelope's house. The swineherd was to tell her privately that Telemachus had returned home safely.

After Eumaeus left, Athena whispered to Odysseus that it was now time to reveal himself to his son. She touched Odysseus with her golden wand and changed him back to his normal self. His handsome and youthful look returned.

Telemachus's eyes grew wide. "I don't understand," he said. "Who are you? How did you suddenly change? Are you a god?"

"I am your father," Odysseus said, "for whom you have suffered for many years." He looked upon Telemachus with a tear in his eye.

It took a few moments for Telemachus to

believe this was his father. He was overcome by sadness and joy, all at once. Soon the great distance he felt toward his father disappeared. It was as if twenty years had not separated them. Telemachus ran to Odysseus and hugged him tightly. He cried as if he were a young boy again. Odysseus lifted his son into the air and laughed.

"Father!" Telemachus shouted. "I have waited ages to see you again. I thought you would never come home. You must have so many stories to tell Mother and me." He smiled. "I cannot wait to hear all of them!"

Odysseus cleared his throat. "My son," he said, "this will all happen in good time. We will have years to get to know each other again. But you must know there is business to be done. You and I must punish the suitors who have troubled your mother. Together we must take back our home."

"But we are only two men," Telemachus replied.

"I know Athena and Zeus will help us," Odysseus told him. "They helped me during my long journey home. The fair gods are on our side. Now go back home without me. Slip in quietly if you can. When you see the suitors, behave just as you did before. Later, I will come to the house disguised again as a beggar. When the suitors mistreat me, be strong. Try not to lose your temper. But try to convince them to be kinder to me. They will get what they deserve in the end.

"Then," Odysseus continued, "collect all the armor and weapons in the house. Hide them in the storage room. But leave a sword and set of armor for each of us. We will need them for the fight. When I nod, it will be our secret signal. That is when we fight. I will set up everything else in the meantime.

"Most importantly," Odysseus said, "tell no one that I am back—not even your mother."

❧

Telemachus had tried his best to return to Ithaca quietly. But the entire household heard of Telemachus's safe arrival. Penelope did not believe it. She needed to see her son to know he was still alive and well.

The suitors were shocked and angry to learn Telemachus was back, and safe. They immediately called a meeting to discuss their situation. One of the strongest suitors was the first to speak.

"My friends," he said, "this is very serious indeed. Somehow Telemachus got past our ship as he came back to Ithaca. We must quickly get word to the ship's crew. They must return here at once."

He had hardly finished speaking when he saw the suitors' ship through the window. The men were pulling into the harbor and lowering the sails. Those men soon returned to Odysseus's house.

When all the suitors were together again, they held another meeting. "I am done with dealing with Telemachus," one of the suitors said. "We must do something to get rid of him. With Telemachus still here, none of us will ever marry Penelope!"

Then a very unusual thing happened. Penelope came down the stairs into the courtyard where the men were meeting. She looked beautiful, with her hair flowing long and shiny. She was wearing a blue gown that shimmered as she stepped into the sunlight. Although she rarely left her room, she had overheard the suitors plotting to kill Telemachus.

Penelope was still beautiful. But sadness and

worry had clearly left their marks upon her face.
First, her husband had been gone for so many
years. Then her son went away without telling
her. Penelope was weary with concern.

"Odysseus was a good and kind leader to you
all!" she scolded them. "How can you destroy

my husband's property, stalk me endlessly, and now plot the death of my son? Shame on you!"

The smoothest talker of all the suitors approached Penelope. He promised her that no harm would come to Telemachus. But really he was the biggest plotter of all. He wanted Telemachus gone more than anyone. Still, his words comforted Penelope. She went back upstairs.

CHAPTER 11

The Hero Comes Home

൧

Athena turned Odysseus back into a beggar because Eumaeus was bound to return soon. Telemachus stood to leave Eumaeus's hut. Odysseus had told him all he needed for the revenge plot. It was time Telemachus finally went home.

"I must show myself to Mother," Telemachus explained. "She must be worried sick. She will not believe I am safe until she has seen me with her own eyes."

Telemachus made his way home. When he

arrived, the old family nurse was the first to spot him. She cried happy tears and shouted for joy. All the other maids came running. So did his mother, Penelope.

When Penelope saw him, she cried hardest of all. "Telemachus! The light of my eyes and beat of my heart!" she said to him, smiling through her tears. "I thought I was never going to see you again."

Then her mood suddenly changed. She stopped hugging him. "Bad boy!" she scolded. "How could you go off without asking my permission?"

But then she softened again and hugged him. "My sweet, wonderful boy—you are back!"

When the suitors saw Telemachus again, they greeted him politely. But this was absolutely false. They wanted to kill him, and Penelope knew it.

Telemachus ignored the men and went to the dining room to celebrate his return. Some of Telemachus's old friends were invited to feast with him. They had a lovely time, eating and drinking. Telemachus was happy to be home. He didn't realize how much he had missed his mother.

This reminded Telemachus he hadn't seen her since the afternoon. He decided to go look for her. Penelope was lying in her usual place, her couch upstairs. She was crying for her missing husband.

"Oh, my son," she said. "I am sorry if I seem ungrateful. I am truly so glad to have you back! But you have said nothing about your father. Did you not find him? I can only assume that he is dead."

Telemachus did not want to see his mother suffer. But she could not know that Odysseus was alive. He had instructed Telemachus not to say a word about his return.

"Mother," he said, "all I can tell you is this: I heard that the old man of the sea saw Father on an island. He was in the cave of the goddess Calypso. She was keeping him prisoner, but he was alive.

"And I have a good feeling that Father has escaped that cave. The gods are on our side, as they have been in the past." Penelope was slightly calmed by her son's words.

Meanwhile, the suitors were downstairs getting ready for another feast. They had just ordered some of Odysseus's best sheep and cows for their meal. The suitors' favorite servant was at the edge of Odysseus's property. He was driving the animals down toward the house. Eumaeus and a disguised Odysseus saw him. The three men met in the meadow.

"Eumaeus," the servant said rudely, "who is this dusty old beggar with you—one of your pigs? Go away! Don't disturb the suitors during their feast."

The servant passed Odysseus and kicked him. But Odysseus stood firm. He didn't fall down like an old, fragile beggar would have. The servant snickered at him. Odysseus controlled his temper. It was not yet time.

Eumaeus and Odysseus made their way to the gate of the house. They paused there. Some music had just started to play.

Eumaeus led the way into the courtyard. The suitors were gathered there. Odysseus followed, looking like a miserable old beggar. He leaned on his cane. His clothes were dirty and in rags. Odysseus wandered slowly among the suitors. Nobody recognized him. He stretched out his hands and begged them for food.

Odysseus stopped in front of one of the bigger suitors. "Sir," he said. "You appear to be a leader among these men. Are you also the most generous? I was once a rich man, too. I used to give to many a beggar, but now I am one."

The suitor scowled. He wrinkled his nose as if Odysseus smelled bad. He said, "Go away, you disgusting man, before you make us lose our appetites."

Odysseus stood up straight. "Your looks, sir, are much better than your manners," he said. "I know that the bread you are eating is not even your own. You are worse than a beggar—you are a *thief*!"

The suitor burned with anger. He picked up a footstool and threw it at Odysseus, hitting his shoulder. Telemachus rose quickly to defend his father. But Odysseus stood firm. He signaled to Telemachus that he must also hold his temper— for now.

Penelope was furious when her servants told her what the reckless suitor had done. "Go and tell the stranger to come here," she demanded. "I want to apologize to him for how he has been treated in my home. Perhaps he is also a traveler and has news of my husband."

However, Odysseus did not come immediately. He sent a message back instead.

Please be patient and wait until sundown. I will come and see you then. I will tell you what I know about your husband.

CHAPTER 12

Odysseus Shows His Strength

Odysseus was dressed as a beggar, in disguise in his own house. However, in Ithaca there was another beggar who was very well known. He begged all over the city.

On this day, he happened to wander into the courtyard where the suitors were feasting. The beggar saw Odysseus and tried to chase him away. "There is only room for one beggar in this city!" he cried.

Of course, the suitors thought this was extremely funny. They gathered around the two beggars. They yelled, "Fight! Fight!" The winner of the beggar's match would be invited to join their feast.

Odysseus agreed to fight as long as Telemachus was referee. He said this would make sure the fight was fair. Odysseus pulled off his shirt of rags to prepare for the match. Everyone was amazed and confused. His chest was strong and mighty. His shoulders and arms were muscular. He did not look like a beggar.

When the beggar saw him, he became nervous. He tried to back out of the fight. The suitors forced him back into the center of the courtyard. They chanted "Fight! Fight!" until the two beggars began throwing punches.

Odysseus easily won. To be kind, he had given the beggar only a gentle hit. Even so, the beggar was too scared to do anything but lie on the ground. The fight was soon over. Odysseus put his shirt of rags back on.

The suitors congratulated him. They kept their promise. Odysseus sat down with them. They offered him food and drink.

While the men ate downstairs, Penelope was upstairs. She nervously paced back and forth. Her servants had told her about the "Battle of the Beggars." It made her angry that this was happening in her home. She wanted to go downstairs and take control back. She also wanted to warn Telemachus that the suitors meant to harm him.

Penelope decided to go downstairs to the suitors' feast. When she entered the courtyard, all the suitors looked up. They gasped. Athena had cast a spell to make Penelope look even more beautiful. The goddess wanted Odysseus and Telemachus to see how Penelope was prized by others.

Penelope stood at the edge of the courtyard. The suitors fell even more deeply in love. They were enchanted by her. Penelope's husband and son definitely noticed their behavior.

One of the suitors approached her. "Queen Penelope. If all the men on the island could see you now, you would have even *more* suitors in your house. You are even lovelier than you were before."

To this, Penelope replied, "Heaven robbed me of my loveliness when my husband was taken from me." The suitor shrank back a little. Athena's spell, it seemed, had also made Penelope brave.

"Telemachus," she said, spotting her son. "How could you let this beggar be so poorly treated in our house?"

Telemachus nodded. "You are right, Mother," he said. "But I am not a little boy anymore. I am a man. And men do not behave perfectly all the time."

Next, Penelope turned to the group of suitors.

"And you," she said, "with all your adoration for me. What have you ever done for me? All you ever do is take things from my home. You all should be more respectful and generous. Why haven't you brought me any gifts?"

Instead of being jealous, Odysseus was actually quite proud of his wife. *Good for her!* he thought. *Let her get back some of the value these thieves have taken from our home!*

One of the suitors stepped forth and said, "Queen Penelope, take as much as you please from us. We will bring you gifts today. But we will not leave here until you have married one of us. Decide who it shall be."

Penelope nodded, and the gifts started to come. Each suitor sent his servant to fetch something for her. Some brought her beautiful dresses. Others brought her valuable gold. Soon she had a pile of pretty things in front of her. She gathered them and went back to her room.

The suitors started celebrating. They sang and danced in the courtyard until the sun set. They felt encouraged by Penelope. She had taken their gifts and seemed pleased. The men lit a bonfire, and sang and danced through the night.

Odysseus joined them, trying to blend in. But Athena was watching the whole time. She was getting impatient. Athena wanted Odysseus to get his revenge on the suitors. She thought he was just wasting time. Athena even tried to stir up a fight between one of the suitors and Odysseus. But Telemachus broke up that fight. And Odysseus was resolved to wait until the right time to attack.

The tired suitors eventually went to bed for the night. Revenge, it seemed, would have to wait another day.

CHAPTER 13

Odysseus Is the Eagle

Telemachus went to bed. He was worn out from the day. He couldn't believe that just that morning, he had arrived on Ithaca's shores. So much had happened. But best of all, Telemachus was reunited with his father. He went to bed happy with this knowledge.

Odysseus walked slowly upstairs to Penelope's rooms. Her maids announced him, and she let him in. Odysseus found her sitting by the fire, looking as lovely as a goddess. He bowed his head to her, since she was royalty and he was disguised as a beggar.

"Please," she said to Odysseus, "sit down. Tell me about yourself. Where are you from? Who is your family?"

"Dear Queen," he responded. "Please ask me any other question. Those memories will only make me weep."

"Oh, stranger," Penelope replied. "How I understand! You see, I lost everything when my husband set sail to fight in the Trojan War. Until he comes back, my sadness will continue."

There, by the fire, Penelope told Odysseus all about the suitors. She told him how they were trying to win her love and wasting her husband's wealth. "I even came up with tricks to delay them," she said. "I sewed a large tapestry every day. I promised to marry one of them when I was finished. But I unraveled my work every night."

"That was a good idea," Odysseus said, nodding.

"It was," Penelope agreed, "until one of my disloyal maids told the suitors what I was doing. Now, sadly, I am out of ideas." She smiled. "But come now, I have told you my own sad story. Won't you tell me yours?"

Odysseus answered, "Madam, I would prefer to tell you this: I once met your husband when he was on his way to Troy. I found him to be an excellent man."

Penelope was excited to hear any news about Odysseus. But she did not completely trust this stranger. So she tested him. Penelope asked him to describe the clothes Odysseus had been wearing. He did this, and even described the cloak she had given her husband. Penelope began to cry.

"Dear Queen," Odysseus continued, "do not cry. I have also heard news of your husband. He is possibly alive and on his way home. It is said he is bringing back great treasures from his travels. These things will be enough to replace all the wealth the suitors have stolen."

This news calmed Penelope. She decided to ask the stranger for his opinion about something.

"I had a dream," she explained. "Twenty geese were wandering around our property. But then a great eagle swooped down from the mountain. The eagle killed the geese and flew away. In the dream, I worried and cried. My maids all gathered around me. Then the eagle came back. It said to me, 'Do not cry. This is not a dream, it's a vision. I am not an eagle. I am your husband, Odysseus. I am coming back to you. I will punish the suitors.'

"When I woke up," Penelope finished, "my geese were wandering around the property, as usual." She paused. "What do you think this dream means?"

Odysseus smiled. "Well, I am no dream

expert. But I think the dream explains itself. Odysseus is the eagle who will destroy all of your suitors, who are the geese. Now, will you promise to stop being so sad?"

Penelope thanked the stranger and promised she would try. Deep down, though, she didn't believe in dreams. She thought they were unsure things. Penelope was the type of woman who took matters into her own hands. And that, she resolved, was exactly what she would do. But not tonight.

"I could sit here and talk with you forever," she told the stranger. "You feel strangely familiar to me. I am very comfortable around you. But I need to get some rest. Let me call one of my maids to make up a guest room for you."

Odysseus then surprised Penelope. He asked that an older, respectable woman prepare his guest room. He did not want a pretty young maid.

Penelope told him that the faithful old family nurse was such a woman. The old nurse had been in the house the night Odysseus was born, many years ago. She was the most respected in the house.

"She sounds perfect," Odysseus said. He wished Penelope a good night. The old nurse entered the room. When she saw the stranger by the fire, her emotions were stirred. He reminded her of Odysseus. Of course, Odysseus was happy to see his old nurse. She had aged much while he was away. He looked fondly upon her, but did not reveal himself.

The old nurse brought Odysseus to his guest room. While he changed into bedclothes, she dressed the bed with clean linens. Odysseus began to climb into bed with the help of the old nurse. As he did, the leg of his pants lifted just slightly. They revealed the scar on his ankle.

The old nurse immediately recognized his

scar. It was the scar given to Odysseus by a wild boar while he was hunting with his grandfather. Only one person in the world could have had it. The nurse gasped.

"Could it be?" she whispered. The nurse leaned down and looked straight into Odysseus's eyes. She began to cry joyful tears. "You *are* my boy!" she said. "Odysseus has returned!"

Odysseus whispered back, "Yes, Nurse, it is me. But please do not say another word. I must stay in disguise." The nurse promised she would not say a word. She did not even ask for a reason.

"Good night, dear master," the nurse said.

"Good night, dear Nurse," replied Odysseus.

Odysseus could not sleep that night. He lay in bed, thinking about his revenge upon the suitors. He felt like growling like an angry dog. He tossed and turned. Suddenly Athena appeared by his side as a woman. She spoke to him in a soothing voice.

"Poor, unhappy man. Why do you lie awake? You are back in your house. Your wife is safe inside it. And your son is a young man any father could be proud of."

Odysseus sighed. "All of that is true," he said. "But I cannot see how we are going to defeat these suitors. They are so many and we are so few."

"Shame on you," Athena scolded him gently. "Am I not a goddess? Have I not protected you through all of your troubles? Even if there were fifty armies of suitors, you would still win with my help. But you need your rest. So shut your eyes now and go to sleep."

Odysseus and Telemachus met early the next morning, before the suitors arrived. Odysseus had dreamed overnight of a way to perfect their plan. The father and son sat in private discussion.

"As I said before, you must gather all of the armor in the house. Take all the helmets, shields, and spears down into the storage room. The suitors will not be able to reach for them there," Odysseus instructed his son. "And what is your excuse when the suitors ask what you are doing?"

"I will say I am cleaning the armor," Telemachus replied.

"Good," Odysseus replied. "And don't forget about our signal to fight."

The suitors started to arrive. They decided to have a giant feast. Penelope would soon be selecting one of them to marry. This called for a celebration.

The entire house prepared for the feast. The maids cleaned and cooked. Even some of the lazy suitors chopped firewood. It was so busy in the house that nobody noticed Telemachus collecting all the armor. He had no problem hiding it in the storage room. Only he and his mother had the key to this room in the palace.

The swineherd, Eumaeus, was called to

bring three of his best pigs. When he arrived, he dropped the pigs off in the kitchen. Then he approached Odysseus, who was still disguised as a beggar. Eumaeus quietly asked how the suitors were treating him.

"Things are calm now," Odysseus replied. "But the excitement is about to begin."

The meal was ready and everyone went inside to eat, including Odysseus. It could have been a pleasant party. But the suitors continued their bad behavior during the feast.

One of the suitors said, "I think we should give this beggar a gift. It should be something fitting for him. Let's give him something he can use to show off."

The nasty suitor picked up a chicken bone and threw it at Odysseus. The mean young man was trying to hit him in the head, but he missed. The other suitors laughed.

Telemachus spoke fiercely to the one who

threw the bone. "It is a good thing for you," he said, "that you missed. Otherwise you would be very sorry. Sir, you are a visitor in my house. Behave yourself!"

He turned to speak to all of the suitors. "I want you all to hear me now," he said. "I am not a child anymore. I have watched you take advantage of my home. In the past, I have been unwilling to fight you. You are many men and I am only one."

He took a deep breath. "But I am done. I have had enough. I will fight the next one who dares to cross me."

The suitors were stunned. They had never heard Telemachus speak so bravely. Suddenly they were overcome with a very strong sense of fear. Athena had thrown this feeling over them like a blanket. But the suitors did not know this. They thought that Telemachus's words had stirred their fear.

CHAPTER 14

The Trial of the Axes

Penelope had given the matter much thought. As much as it pained her, she decided her husband must be dead. There was no way he was coming back. She had to move on with her life. She had to choose one of the suitors to marry.

Penelope decided she would hold a contest—a test of skill for the suitors. She took a small key out from her secret hiding place. She went into the storage room and found what she was looking for. Leaning against the wall was an old, spare bow of her husband's, and a bag full of arrows.

Penelope walked into the courtyard where the suitors had gathered after eating. Her maids followed behind her. She reached the center of the circle of men and cleared her throat to make an announcement.

"Since it seems you will not give up," she said loudly, "I finally have. Although I will never forget my husband, I will marry one of you."

The suitors cheered. Penelope raised her hand to stop them. "Not so fast," she said. "I am not finished. I will marry the one of you who can pass this test. String this bow and send an arrow flying in a straight line. It must fly through the holes of twelve axes. I shall arrange these axes so they stand up in a straight line on the ground."

The suitors were excited for the challenge. Telemachus didn't like it, but it was clear his mother was insistent. He was also certain that his father would somehow manage to compete with the suitors. Odysseus would surely beat them all. "Come on, then!" Telemachus said. "Let us get this contest started."

The suitors cheered, ready to play. Penelope arranged the axes upright in a straight line on the ground. The holes of the axes were lined up perfectly. All the suitors had to do was shoot the arrow straight through the twelve holes. To Telemachus, it looked easy. He tried first to complete the task, to see if it could be done. But he could barely even string the bow.

One after the other, the suitors took their turns with the bow. Some tried warming the bow or softening it with grease to make it easier. But most of the suitors were not strong enough to string the bow. This meant they could not even try to shoot the arrow through the axes.

The last two suitors to try were the most

outspoken and bold. These two men thought they would have no problem completing the challenge. They each bent down to string the bow. Both of them struggled.

While the group was distracted, Odysseus stepped out of the courtyard. He asked Eumaeus and another loyal farmhand, Philoetius, to join him.

Odysseus asked them, "If somehow Odysseus were to come back today to challenge the suitors, would you stand by him?"

They both said "yes" right away. Odysseus told them who he was. "It is I," he said, "your Odysseus. I have suffered much. I have traveled for a long time. Finally, after twenty years, I am back in my own country."

As proof, Odysseus showed them the scar on his leg. Even though he was still disguised as the beggar, the two men recognized his scar. Just like the old nurse had, the men threw their arms around Odysseus. They cried with joy and relief at his return.

"Enough," Odysseus said gently. "Let us go back now. I know the suitors will try to stop me. But I want to take my turn stringing that bow."

Odysseus instructed Eumaeus to send all of the women, except Penelope, upstairs to a safe place. He explained that a battle might occur. If so, it would be dangerous.

"The women must not come back downstairs, even if they hear an uproar," he said. "And lock the doors of the courtyard. None of the suitors should be able to get out."

The men went off to complete their tasks. Odysseus returned to the courtyard.

Meanwhile, the suitors were still trying to string the bow. One of them was warming it by the fire. Even though he was the strongest of all the suitors, he could not string it, either. He looked very frustrated.

"I don't even mind that I can't marry Penelope," he confessed. "What I mind is that Odysseus strung this bow, and we cannot!"

Odysseus, still disguised, had made his way back into the courtyard. He walked over to the row of axes.

"Let me try my hand at this challenge," he said to the suitors.

The men laughed at him, but nervously. After all, it would be humiliating if this beggar could string the bow.

One of the suitors spoke. "Wretched creature," he said. "Why even bother? Even if you string it, do you really think the fair Penelope would ever choose you?"

"I would not," said Penelope. "So what is the harm in letting him try, just for fun?"

"But what if he succeeds?" the suitor asked. "Imagine the gossip that would spread through the town. We would be shamed!"

Penelope answered, "People who dishonor the home of a great king should not care about gossip or shame. Give the beggar the bow. If he can string it, I will give him clean clothes and sandals, and send him on his way. If he can shoot the arrow through the axes, he will have the honor of completing the challenge."

Finally, the suitors agreed. They gave Odysseus the bow. The moment it touched his hands, Odysseus handled it easily. He strung it quickly. He plucked the string to test it. It rang with a grim tone.

The suitors watched, silent and pale. Odysseus took an arrow to the bow. He aimed and took his shot. That arrow flew straight through all twelve holes in the axes. Penelope was impressed. She congratulated the stranger and ran upstairs to tell the other women.

At that moment, Odysseus nodded to his son. This was the signal to begin their fight.

Telemachus sprang into action immediately. He grabbed his sword and spear, and leaped to his father's side.

Odysseus tore off his rags. The beggar whom the suitors had abused turned into the king, Odysseus. He was as strong and swift as they had remembered him to be. The suitors watched with shock and horror.

Odysseus crouched down low to quickly restring his bow. The suitors sprang up and scrambled to grab their own weapons and shields. But their armor had been removed from the courtyard. The suitors ran for the gate, but it had been locked.

"Is it clear yet who I am?" Odysseus roared. "I am the one and only Odysseus. You have wasted my wealth and tried to win my wife's heart. I have come to take my revenge upon you all!"

The suitors begged Odysseus for forgiveness. "If you *are* Odysseus," they said, "then you have a right to be angry. But we will pay you back. We will give you even more wealth than we have wasted from your home."

Odysseus shook his head. "No, sirs," he said. "It is I who shall repay you with my bow and arrows."

One by one, the disloyal suitors fell at the hands of Odysseus and Telemachus. Father and son fought bravely together. They had much help from Odysseus's trusted friends, Eumaeus and Philoetius. Still, the suitors were many men and Odysseus's group was only a few. But the gods were on their side, as Athena had promised. She even fought alongside them when they had trouble. After a long and grueling fight, Odysseus had taken his final revenge. All the suitors had fallen.

When the battle was over, Odysseus's home was entirely his again. His triumph felt unlike any other. Odysseus embraced his son, and thanked his loyal friends for their help.

Then he called his old nurse down to the courtyard. She arrived and saw the suitors lying dead on the ground.

"Master, what has happened?" said the nurse.

"I have gotten rid of the suitors. Go to Penelope. Tell her the truth about me," said Odysseus. It was time to win back his wife.

CHAPTER 15

Penelope and Odysseus Meet Again

~⌒~

In her excitement, the nurse's old feet became young and quick again. She sprinted upstairs to tell her mistress the news.

"My lady," the nurse cried. "Odysseus has returned. He has destroyed the suitors! We are now free."

"My good nurse," answered Penelope, "have you lost your mind? Don't punish me like this. I have finally stopped crying over my lost husband. Are you trying to trick me?"

"My dear," the nurse said. "I promise I am

not trying to trick you. Remember the stranger you welcomed into your home? The one who just shot his arrow through the axes? That was Odysseus!"

Penelope suddenly realized it might be true. She jumped up from her bed and began pacing her room. Penelope trusted her nurse, but she was still uncertain. This was a truth she wanted to believe so much.

"I can give you proof," the nurse said. "I saw his scar! I wanted to tell you about it, but he would not let me. Now he has asked that I reveal the truth to you."

This was excellent proof, but Penelope was still unsure. "Bring him here," she said. The nurse happily ran from the room to fetch her master.

When Odysseus arrived, Penelope kept her distance. He looked like her husband. But she could not be sure this was not an awful test from the gods. Penelope carefully came close to him. They sat by the fire with some distance still between them.

Then Telemachus leaped into the room. He was excited about the reunion of his parents after twenty years. But he was upset that they still sat so far apart.

"Mother," he cried. "Do you not recognize your husband? Why do you not go to him? Is your heart made of stone?"

Penelope answered, "My son, there are things you do not yet understand. If he really is my husband, Odysseus, we will need some time to get to know each other again."

Odysseus smiled and said to Telemachus, "Let her test me. Your mother's cleverness is one of the things I love about her. She will make up her own mind. Just give her time. Besides, I have more awful things to worry about. The suitors' families will surely be greatly upset. We will need to lie low for a while. Telemachus, please go and have the servants secure the house. I will stay here with your mother." Telemachus went and did as his father had asked.

Penelope thought for a moment before speaking again. She rose and moved toward her bed. "I was wondering if you could help me with something," she said to Odysseus. "This bed that I once shared with my husband has moved a bit too close to the window. I would like to move it, but it is too heavy. Can you help?"

Odysseus smiled. "Why, Penelope, I would be glad to help you. But as you know, that bed is not movable. It is made out of a thick tree trunk that grew up through the center of our house. I built it with my own hands. This was a secret between us."

That is what finally convinced Penelope. No one else could have known the bed's history but Odysseus. With this proof, Penelope rejoiced.

She ran to Odysseus and threw her arms around him. He hugged her back as tightly as he could.

"Do not be angry with me," she begged. "I just needed to be sure you were truly Odysseus."

"My dear and faithful wife," Odysseus replied. "The sight of you is as welcome as the sight of land to a shipwrecked man."

Then the couple talked and laughed until morning. Penelope told Odysseus about her suffering at the hands of the wicked suitors. And Odysseus, in his turn, told her how he had suffered at sea.

He told her about the lotus eaters on the island, and how his men gave in to eating the plants. He told her the story of how he had blinded the Cyclops. He told her about Circe, the goddess who had put a spell on him and his men. Then he told her about his travels to Hades to consult the prophet Teiresias. With sadness, he described seeing the ghost of his mother.

He told her about the tempting song of the Sirens. He also could not forget the story of the terrible Scylla, who feasted upon passing travelers with her many heads. He spoke of how his men stole the cattle of the Sun God, even though they were warned not to. He shivered when he told Penelope how Zeus punished them, striking their ships with a lightning bolt. Odysseus told his wife about the goddess Calypso.

"She wanted to make me immortal," he

explained, "so that I would never grow old. She wanted me to stay with her forever."

"And why didn't you let her?" Penelope asked.

"Because I want to grow old with *you*," Odysseus answered.

Later that morning, Odysseus was feeling better than he had in twenty years. He was overjoyed to be with Penelope and Telemachus again.

It was now time for Odysseus to see his father, Laertes, again. Having met his mother in Hades, he was nervous to see his father. Odysseus could not imagine what time might have done to Laertes. The old man did not know his son was still alive.

Odysseus prepared for a long walk in the woods. His old father had moved to the forest once his wife had passed away and Odysseus had gone missing.

Arriving at the cabin in the woods, Odysseus

found his father out in the garden. The old man looked old and weary. He wore patched and shabby clothing. Odysseus felt like crying.

"Excuse me, sir," Odysseus said. "I see that you are an excellent gardener. But it seems that you take better care of your garden than of yourself. Why do you look so worn down? And can you tell me if this is Ithaca, where my good friend Odysseus used to live?"

Laertes answered the second question first. "Sir, this is indeed Ithaca. It is where your friend—and my beloved son—Odysseus used to live. But alas, my poor son has died. My grief has made me old and tired."

This was enough for Odysseus. He jumped toward his father and kissed him on both cheeks.

"Father," he said, "it is me, Odysseus! Look—I have this scar to prove it." He showed the scar to his father. "This came from a wild boar tusk. It happened many years ago, when I was out hunting with my grandfather." Then Odysseus walked through the garden and pointed out all of his father's favorite flowers. He recited the names of all the trees. Finally, Laertes recognized his son.

"You have made an old man happier than you can imagine," Laertes said. And he gave his long-lost son a hug.

***

While Odysseus journeyed into the woods, the fallen suitors were on a journey of their own. Hermes had led their ghosts down to Hades.

The other ghosts in Hades came quickly to greet the suitors. They were shocked to see so many there all at once. The old ghosts demanded to know what had happened.

One of the suitor ghosts answered, "Odysseus was gone for twenty years. We tried to charm his wife and steal his property. He came back and got his revenge."

Another suitor ghost spoke up. He was angry. "We may be down here, but we were the sons of the finest men in Ithaca. Word will quickly spread about what has happened. Odysseus will be punished!"

The suitor ghosts were right. Word spread quickly about what Odysseus had done. There were calls for more fighting and more revenge—this time upon Odysseus. But Ithaca's wisest, oldest man and prophet stood before the people.

"Hear me, men of Ithaca," he said. "Odysseus did not do these things against the will of the gods. It is our own fault these things happened. We let the suitors remain in Odysseus's house. We didn't help Penelope and Telemachus. The anger and revenge have to stop. They must stop here, and now."

Not everyone agreed with the old man. It took a little extra help from the gods to make peace. Athena hovered above Ithaca and cast her most powerful spell of all—a spell of forgiveness and friendship.

With this, peace in Ithaca was finally restored.

What Do *You* Think?
Questions for Discussion

⁓

Have you ever been around a toddler who keeps asking the question "Why?" Does your teacher call on you in class with questions from your homework? Do your parents ask you about your day at the dinner table? We are always surrounded by questions that need a specific response. But is it possible to have a question with no right answer?

The following questions are about the

book you just read. But this is not a quiz! They are designed to help you look at the people, places, and events in the story from different angles. These questions do not have specific answers. Instead, they might make you think of the story in a completely new way.

Think carefully about each question and enjoy discovering more about this classic story.

1. How do the gods guide the human characters in *The Odyssey*? How do they punish them? Which of the gods is your favorite? Which is your least favorite?

2. While Odysseus is away, his house is filled with men who want to marry Penelope. How do these suitors behave? Do you think that they care about Penelope? If you were Penelope, would you want to marry one of them?

3. The goddess Calypso traps Odysseus on her island so he will stay with her forever. Even

though it is a paradise, Odysseus wants to go home. How would you feel if you were on this island? Would you want to go home, too?

4. What happens when the Cyclops finally finds out it was Odysseus who blinded him? How does the Cyclops find this out? How does that event affect Odysseus for the rest of his journey?

5. When Odysseus hears the Sirens' song, what is it like? Why does he listen to it? Have you ever done something you knew was bad for you? Did your friends help you out of trouble, as Odysseus's men did by tying their leader to the mast?

6. Is Odysseus a good storyteller? Would you want to go with him on an adventure? Out of all his adventures, which is your favorite?

7. When Odysseus returns to Ithaca, he disguises himself as a beggar and keeps his true identity a secret from everyone, even Penelope. Can you think of a time when you had to

keep a secret? Was it difficult to do? If you were Odysseus, would you have been able to pretend that you didn't know your friends and family?

8. Odysseus's friends and family recognize him by the scar on his leg, even when he is in disguise. Do you have any traits such as a scar that would help your friends and family to recognize you?

9. What do you think of Penelope when she finally decides to marry one of the suitors? Do you think it was a good idea to give them the challenge of the axes? If you could pick a challenge for the suitors, what would it be?

10. When Odysseus finally reveals himself to Penelope, she doubts that it is really he. How does he prove himself to Penelope? If you were Penelope, would you have believed Odysseus right away, or would you also need proof?

A Note to Parents and Educators
By Arthur Pober, EdD

ॐ

First impressions are important.

Whether we are meeting new people, going to new places, or picking up a book unknown to us, first impressions can count for a lot. They can lead to warm, lasting memories or can make us shy away from future encounters.

Can you recall your own first impressions and earliest memories of reading the classics?

Do you remember wading through pages and pages of text to prepare for an exam? Or were you the child who hid under the blanket to read with a flashlight, joining forces with Robin Hood to save Maid Marian? Do you remember only how long it took you to read a lengthy novel such as *Little Women*? Or did you become best friends with the March sisters?

Even for a gifted young reader, getting through long chapters with dense language can easily become overwhelming and can obscure the richness of the story and its characters. Reading an abridged, newly crafted version of a classic novel can be the gentle introduction a child needs to explore the characters and story line without the frustrations of difficult vocabulary and complex themes.

Reading an abridged version of a classic novel gives the young reader a sense of independence and the satisfaction of finishing a "grown-up" book. And when a child is engaged with and inspired by a classic story, the tone is set for further exploration of the story's themes, characters, history, and details. As a child's reading skills advance, the desire to tackle the original, unabridged version of the story will naturally emerge.

If made accessible to young readers, these stories can become invaluable tools for understanding themselves in the context of their families and social environments. This is why the Classic Starts series includes questions that stimulate discussion regarding the impact and social relevance of the characters and stories today. These questions can foster lively conversations between children and their parents or teachers. When we look at the issues, values, and standards of past times in terms of how we live now, we can appreciate literature's classic tales in a very personal and engaging way.

Share your love of reading the classics with a young child, and introduce an imaginary world real enough to last a lifetime.

Dr. Arthur Pober, EdD

Dr. Arthur Pober has spent more than twenty years in the fields of early childhood and gifted education. He is the former principal of one of the world's oldest laboratory schools for gifted youngsters, Hunter College Elementary School, and former director of Magnet Schools for the Gifted and Talented for more than twenty-five thousand youngsters in New York City.

Dr. Pober is a recognized authority in the areas of media and child protection and is currently the U.S. representative to the European Institute for the Media and European Advertising Standards Alliance.

Explore these wonderful stories in our
Classic Starts™ Library.